Going to the ZOO

Verse:

1. Dad-dy's tak-ing us to the zoo to-mor-row, zoo to-mor-row,

zoo to-mor-row. Dad-dy's tak-ing us to the zoo to-mor-row.

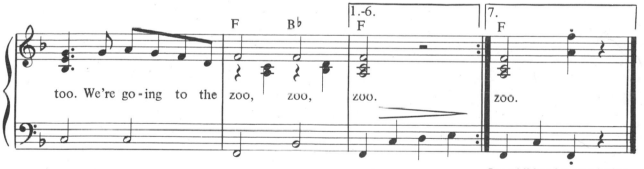

See additional verses inside.

Going to the Zoo

TOM PAXTON

illustrated by
KAREN LEE SCHMIDT

SCHOLASTIC INC.
New York Toronto London
Auckland Sydney Mexico City
New Delhi Hong Kong

ISBN 0-439-08373-7

20 19 18 17 16 15   5 6 7/0

Printed in the U.S.A.   40

First Scholastic printing, May 1999

Watercolor and gouache were used for the full-color illustrations.
The text type is 15-point Versailles.

For Christopher
—T.P.

Daddy's taking us to the zoo tomorrow,
zoo tomorrow, zoo tomorrow.
Daddy's taking us to the zoo tomorrow.
We can stay all day.

We're going to the zoo, zoo, zoo.
How about you, you, you?
You can come too, too, too.
We're going to the zoo, zoo, zoo.

See the elephants with the long trunks swingin',
great big ears and the long trunks swingin',
sniffin' up peanuts with the long trunks swingin'.
We can stay all day.

See all the monkeys scritch, scritch, scratchin',
jumpin' all around and scritch, scritch, scratchin',
hanging by their long tails, scritch, scritch, scratchin'.
We can stay all day.

Big black bear is a-huff, huff, a-puffin',
coat's too heavy, he's a-huff, huff, a-puffin',
don't get too near the huff, huff, a-puffin'.
Or you won't stay all day.

We're going to the zoo, zoo, zoo.
How about you, you, you?
You can come too, too, too.
We're going to the zoo, zoo, zoo.

Kangaroo is a-hop, hop, hoppin',
big long tail is a-flop, flop, floppin',
baby's in the pouch all hop, hop, hoppin'.
We can stay all day.

Seals in the pool, clap, clap, clappin',
catching fish and clap, clap, clappin',
bouncing the ball and clap, clap, clappin'.
We can stay all day.

What's that sound? Lion is a-roarin',
time to eat! Lion is a-roarin',
now lazy Mister Lion is a-snorin'.
We can stay all day.

We're going to the zoo, zoo, zoo.
How about you, you, you?
You can come too, too, too.
We're going to the zoo, zoo, zoo.

Birds in the birdhouse chirpin' and a-cheepin',
flyin' in circles and chirpin' and a-cheepin',
Mister Owl is quietly sleepin'.
We can stay all day.

We stayed all day and we're gettin' sleepy,
sittin' in the backseat, sleep, sleep, sleepy,
home already and we're really sleepy.
We have stayed all day.

We've been to the zoo, zoo, zoo.
So have you, you, you.
You came too, too, too.
We've been to the zoo, zoo, zoo.

Momma's takin' us to the zoo tomorrow!
Zoo tomorrow! Zoo tomorrow!
Momma's takin' us to the zoo tomorrow!
We can stay all day!

We're going to the zoo, zoo, zoo.
How about you, you, you?
You can come too, too, too.
We're going to the zoo, zoo, zoo.

Going to the ZOO

Verse: F ... C7

1. Dad-dy's tak-ing us to the zoo to-mor-row, zoo to-mor-row,

mf

zoo to-mor-row. Dad-dy's tak-ing us to the zoo to-mor-row.

We can stay all day. We're go - ing to the zoo, zoo,

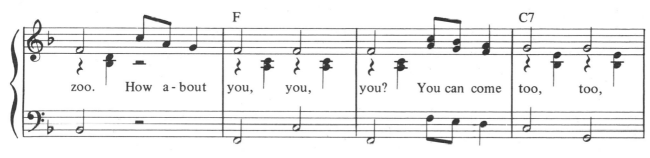

zoo. How a - bout you, you, you? You can come too, too,

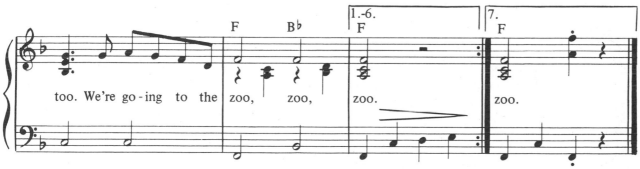

too. We're go - ing to the zoo, zoo, zoo. zoo.

See additional verses inside.